DON'T FEED THE ANIMALS!

ISBN 978-976-96367-0-5

Published by Nadira Green

Scarborough, Tobago.

www.nadiragreen.com

For my son Theodore.

This book belongs to

"Don't feed the animals," exclamation mark, was written on a sign in the Wildlife Park.

Did people listen? No, they did not.
They fed them quite a lot.
WELCOME
DON'T
FEED THE
ANIMALS!

Max the monkey got very fat.

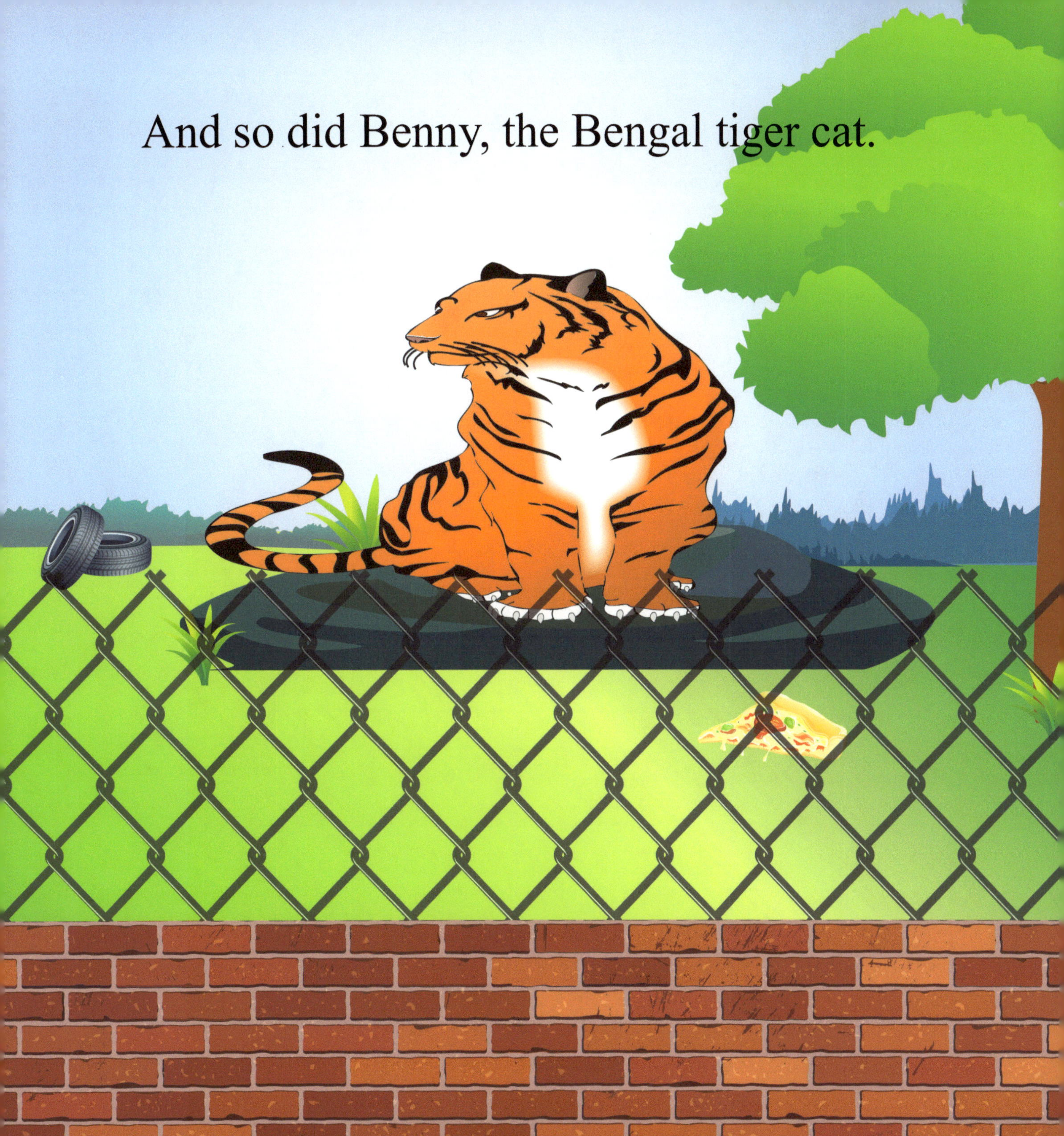
And so did Benny, the Bengal tiger cat.

Louie the lion almost bit someone's hand.

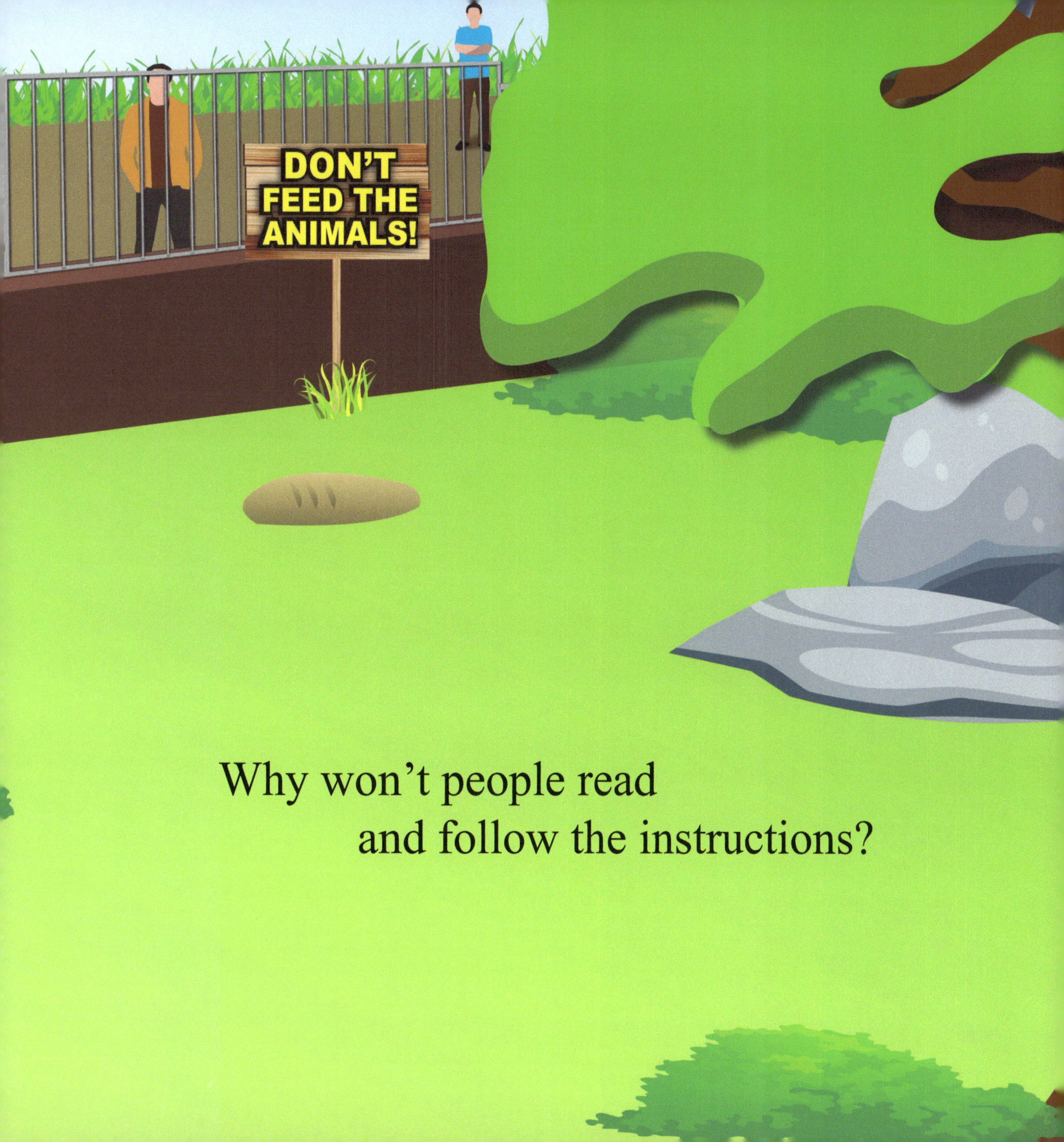

Why won't people read
and follow the instructions?

Ali the alligator almost choked on a shoe.

Then the keepers came to the rescue.
Whew!

Izzie the iguana was fed
fish in her pan.

She got very sick because
it changed her diet plan.

Eva the elephant lost a
lot of weight.

All because she ate fish bait.

Billy the bear
started losing his hair.

It kept falling out everywhere.

"Don't feed the animals!"
The keepers shouted loud and clear.

Maggie the macaw was the very

last straw. The keepers marched
people out the door. One by one
and into a line, for not following
instructions on the sign.

"You need to be trained," the keepers explained. "The animals' health need to be maintained."

So when you visit a zoo or a wildlife park, DON'T FEED THE ANIMALS!

COLOUR ME

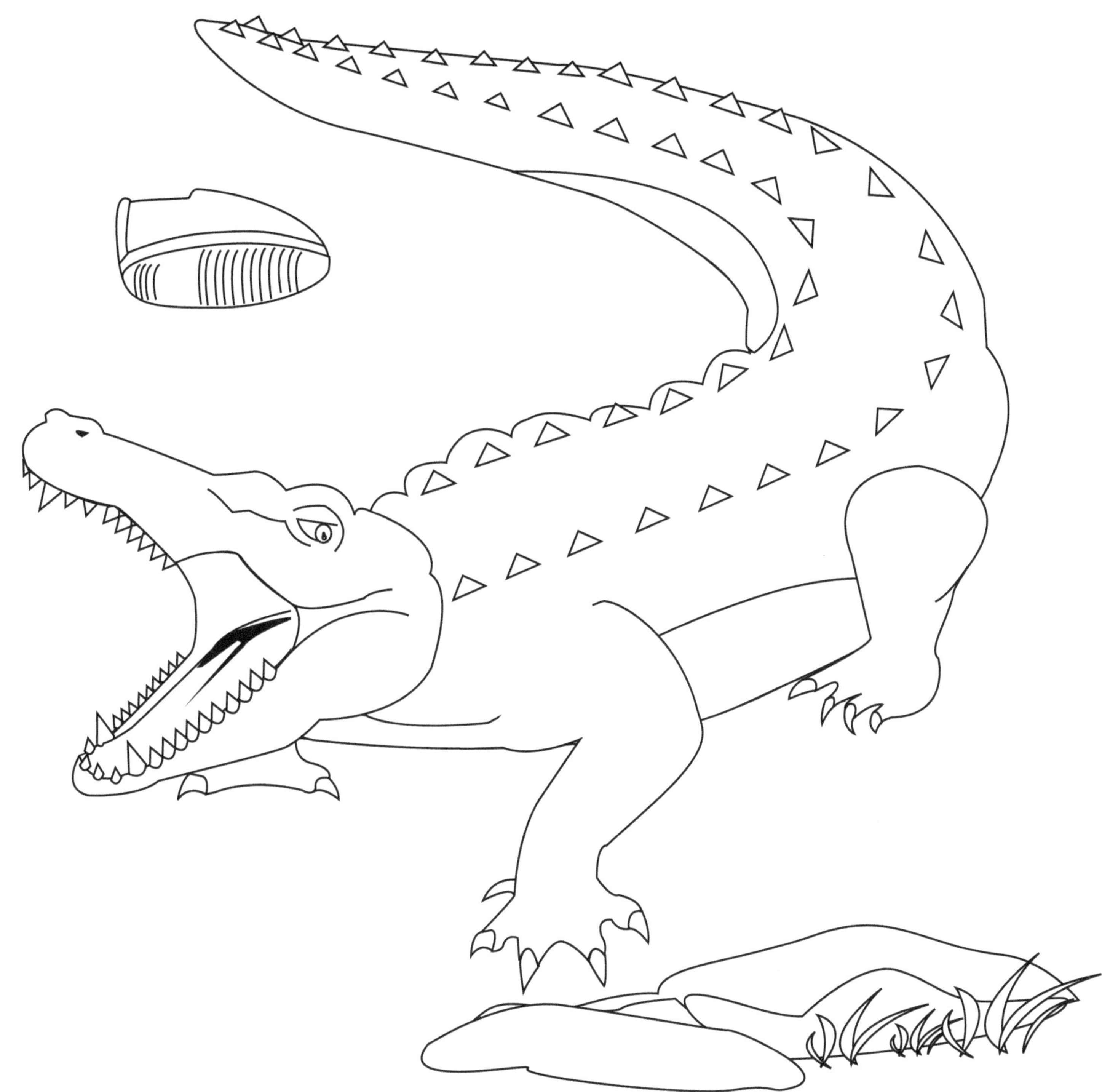

DON'T
FEED THE
ANIMALS!

www.ingramcontent.com/pod-product-compliance
Lightning Source LLC
Chambersburg PA
CBHW042121110726
48006CB00002B/724